JEMMA'S GOT THE TRAVEL BUG

SUSAN GLICK

ILLUSTRATIONS BY KELLI NASH

4880 Lower Valley Road Atglen, PA 19310

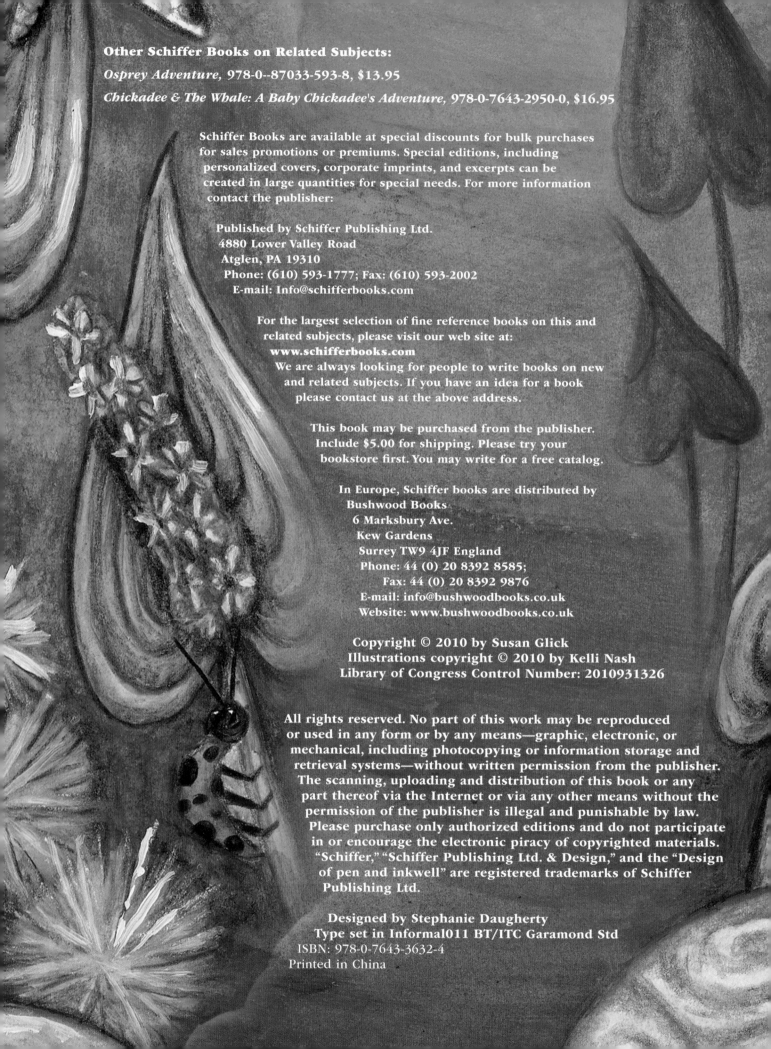

Other Schiffer Books on Related Subjects:
Osprey Adventure, 978-0--87033-593-8, $13.95
Chickadee & The Whale: A Baby Chickadee's Adventure, 978-0-7643-2950-0, $16.95

Schiffer Books are available at special discounts for bulk purchases for sales promotions or premiums. Special editions, including personalized covers, corporate imprints, and excerpts can be created in large quantities for special needs. For more information contact the publisher:

Published by Schiffer Publishing Ltd.
4880 Lower Valley Road
Atglen, PA 19310
Phone: (610) 593-1777; Fax: (610) 593-2002
E-mail: Info@schifferbooks.com

For the largest selection of fine reference books on this and related subjects, please visit our web site at:
www.schifferbooks.com
We are always looking for people to write books on new and related subjects. If you have an idea for a book please contact us at the above address.

This book may be purchased from the publisher.
Include $5.00 for shipping. Please try your bookstore first. You may write for a free catalog.

In Europe, Schiffer books are distributed by
Bushwood Books
6 Marksbury Ave.
Kew Gardens
Surrey TW9 4JF England
Phone: 44 (0) 20 8392 8585;
Fax: 44 (0) 20 8392 9876
E-mail: info@bushwoodbooks.co.uk
Website: www.bushwoodbooks.co.uk

Designed by Stephanie Daugherty
Type set in Informal011 BT/ITC Garamond Std
ISBN: 978-0-7643-3632-4
Printed in China

DEDICATION

For Aunt Norma, who loved a good adventure...

~ Susan Glick

To Tripp & Anna with love...

~ Kelli Nash

ACKNOWLEDGMENTS

Many thanks to the Terrapin Institute's Marguerite Whilden, who kindly answered my many questions as I was researching this book. She has worked tirelessly to educate the public and to protect the diamondback terrapin. ~ SG

Before Jemma got the travel bug, she loved every mud flat, every salt marsh, and every muskrat lodge and fallen tree in her quiet cove by the Chesapeake Bay. The young diamondback terrapin never gave a thought to leaving.

But then the horseshoe crab scuttled by. "Off to the continental shelf," he called out to Jemma.

A little while later, an American eel wiggled past. "Time to swim to the Sargasso Sea," he announced.

Overhead, the osprey circled the cove. "South America, here I come! *Adios*."

Jemma watched her friends scuttle, wiggle, and fly away. She'd been in her quiet cove for six summers and six winters. She wasn't a tiny hatchling anymore. She was ready, she decided, to explore deeper waters.

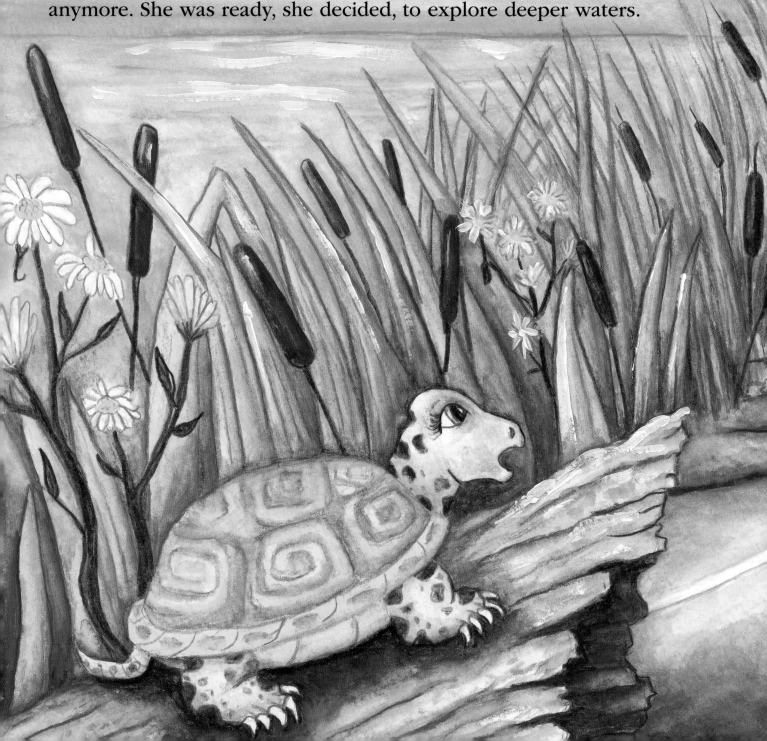

"Wait!" she cried out. "I'm coming, too!"
The travel bug had caught her that quick.
At the mouth of her cove, a big wave lifted
and tossed her into a somersault. Jemma had
to use all four of her webbed feet to steer and
paddle, and before long, she was swimming
up and over, and even under, the waves.

All of this swimming made Jemma hungry. She lifted her speckled head above the swells and looked around for her usual late day snack. Back in the salt marsh, she might have munched on a fiddler crab or crunched on a periwinkle snail. But here the water was dark and deep.

Then Jemma caught a whiff of something deliciously familiar. It was menhaden, an oily little fish that Jemma couldn't resist. She hurried toward a baited crab pot on the Bay floor and scooted in through the narrow opening. "Yum," she said, greedily grabbing her favorite fish in her strong jaws.

Six eyes watched her.

Six claws waved angrily.

Jemma returned to the tight opening and tried and tried to slide her body through. Even though she was a rather smallish turtle, she couldn't get free! She was trapped inside the crab pot!

Jemma was frightened. She knew she could drown if she stayed underwater too long.

Jemma was getting very, very worried, especially when she felt the vibrations of a motor boat above her.

Swoosh.

Up, up, up.

Clunk. The metal pot thudded onto the boat's deck. Jemma took a big gulp of air.

"Only catching crabs today," a whiskery man said, grabbing and tossing her over the side of the boat.

Jemma tumbled.

She flipped.

She spun.

The boat's noisy propellers buzzed and chopped. Jemma's strong back legs were powerless in the churning water.

She had to get away fast! She dove...
down, down, down to the bottom of
the Bay.

When the boat's buzz was off in the distance, Jemma returned to the surface. She swam up, over, and under the waves, feeling all alone in the big water. Her peaceful cove was nowhere in sight.

The osprey was long gone, and so were the horseshoe crab and the American eel. Even with her new swimming skills, Jemma was certain she couldn't paddle to the continental shelf or the Sargasso Sea.

"And South America is out of the question," she admitted. After all, she was just a turtle with a touch of the travel bug.

The days went by. Jemma tried to make the best of her situation.

When she was hungry, she chased down silversides, making sure to stay far away from crab pots.

When she was chilly, she stretched out on the sunny surface of the water to bask.

When she was thirsty, she opened her mouth and captured raindrops as they fell from the sky.

But each night, before she fell asleep, she imagined a place where the air smelled like mud, where the flow of the creek switched direction with the tides, where the marsh grass made crinkly sounds when it blew in the breeze.

Then one day, Jemma saw pine trees along the shoreline. Excited, she paddled closer. She entered a small inlet, where the beaches were gently sloped and sandy, and narrow creeks flowed through the cordgrass. She used her sharp claws to pull herself out of the water.

Jemma sighed contentedly. It felt wonderful to have solid ground under her shell again!

"Hello there," a voice called out from behind her. Perched on a piece of driftwood was a turtle with diamond swirls on his back — just like hers. "My name is Speck," he said.

Together, Jemma and Speck swam in the tidal creeks and munched on worms and periwinkles.

They watched the river otter slide down the mud bank and the blue heron fish on the edge of the marsh.

They basked in the autumn sun.

When the days grew short and their basking pond turned icy, Jemma and Speck and the other terrapins found a mucky creek bed where they could spend the winter.

And Jemma snuggled in next to Speck,
happy to be home from her travels.

ABOUT THE DIAMONDBACK . . .

For Teachers and Parents

Where does the diamondback terrapin live?

The diamondback terrapin, frequently described as "shy" and "elusive," is an aquatic turtle found in salt marshes, estuaries, and tidal creeks from Cape Cod, Massachusetts, to the Gulf of Mexico in Texas. The diamondback is distinguished by the diamond-shaped pattern on its top shell (carapace) and the spotted markings on its head, neck, and feet. The diamondback prefers to live in intertidal zones, not the open waters of bays, although it has occasionally been spotted swimming in the ocean. The diamondback is not, in fact, a big traveler. Rather, it demonstrates "site fidelity," which means most diamondbacks will remain in a location for years if that site provides food and shelter, a place to hibernate, and, for females, a sandy place to deposit eggs.

The diamondback terrapin is the only turtle that lives exclusively in brackish (a mix of fresh and salty) water. The terrapin can be difficult to spot in the marsh, but is often seen swimming on the surface of the water, with only the top of its head visible, looking a little bit like a snake or a stick protruding from the water. When it's approached, it will quickly duck under and hide. During the winter, in northern climates, diamondbacks hibernate by burrowing into a mud bank or creek bed, often in groups.

What does this turtle eat and drink?

Perhaps surprisingly, diamondbacks are not passive eaters, but instead stalk and overtake their prey. They only eat underwater. Diamondbacks have no teeth, but use their strong jaws and sharp claws to break apart their food. They eat periwinkle snails, fiddler crabs, mussels, small fish, worms, and carrion.

While diamondbacks live in brackish water, they need to consume freshwater. Commonly, they drink by lowering their heads in puddles and taking in rainwater through their nostrils. Less often, they simply open their mouths and catch rain.

What threatens a diamondback?

The life of a diamondback is not without its dangers. Terrapins are killed by boat propellers or by dredging machinery. Too often, they suffocate when trapped in crab pots, eel traps, or fishing nets. Abandoned crab pots are a serious hazard for diamondbacks. Over-harvesting is also a threat to the diamondback. Additionally, female terrapins are killed or injured when crossing roads in search of sandy places to deposit their eggs. Very young terrapins, hatchlings, are the most vulnerable. Predators of terrapin nests and young hatchlings include raccoons, rats, foxes, birds (hawks, eagles, crows), and even insects. Finally, the diamondback is in danger of losing its habitat as marshland disappears and sandy beaches are replaced by seawalls and rip rap.